Nicky's Shadow

Nicky's Shadow

RUTH KIRTLEY

Scripture Union
130 City Road, London EC1V 2NJ

© Ruth Kirtley 1988
First published 1988

ISBN 0 86201 476 X

Phototypesetting by Input Typesetting Ltd., London.
Printed by Cox and Wyman Ltd., Reading.

Contents

For Christopher and Peter

Nicky's shadow

Nicky and Mummy were going shopping. They had taken big brother Martin to school and now they were walking down the busy main road into town. The cars and buses were swooshing by and there was lots to look at as they walked along.

Nicky is really Nicholas, but hardly anyone ever calls him by that name. He's quite an ordinary boy; not thin, but then not really fat either. His Grannie says he's 'just comfortable'. He has very curly brown hair and, in the summer, he has freckles on his nose. When these stories begin he's nearly five years old and quite grown up about things like dressing himself and writing his name. He's a very busy boy but he does a lot of thinking too, and he asks a great many questions. Nicky's big brother Martin is eight. He's very tall and he has curly ginger hair. Martin has been at school a long time and he knows *everything*. He and Nicky are good friends most of the time, and Nicky can't wait to go to school like Martin does.

Usually Nicky and Mummy stopped at the motor bike shop to see the row of shining new motor bikes standing outside. Nicky would show Mummy which one he was going to buy when he was grown up. Often he would ask for a ride in the rocket ship that stood outside the toy shop. Sometimes Mummy had the right money and he would climb in and pretend to chase the passing cars as he whirred up and down. When they passed the old folks' flats they would look out for the lady with the two stripey cats. In sunny weather she sat in a chair on her doorstep. She would smile and nod to Mummy and Nicky, and her cats would come purring to meet them. Nicky liked it when they wound round his legs and tickled him with their whiskers.

Today, though, Nicky was too busy to look at motor bikes; he didn't even bother to ask about the rocket-ship and, even though it was sunny, the old lady wasn't on her doorstep, so he didn't need to wave. Nicky was far too busy to do all the usual things because he had discovered his shadow and, ever since he and big brother Martin had left home, he'd been watching it carefully.

He had found that his shadow did everything he did. If Nicky ran, his shadow ran. If he hopped, so did his shadow. Even when he tried to catch his shadow out by turning round quickly, there it was, right beside him, doing just whatever he did. Nicky and his shadow had run races with Martin and *his* shadow. That had been fun, but now Martin had gone to school, taking his Martin-shadow with him, so Nicky was on his own, playing with his Nicky-shadow.

He crouched down small and hopped along the pavement, keeping his eye on his crouched-down shadow, as it hopped along just beside him. 'What on earth are you doing, Nicky?' asked Mummy.

'Watching my shadow. Look, it's all little like me,' said Nicky.

'Well, jump up now and hold my hand while we cross the road,' said Mummy. Nicky bounced over the black and white stripes of the crossing and he didn't let go of Mummy's hand until they were safely on the other side. Then he looked down and gave a yell. 'It's gone!'

'What has, lovey?'

'My shadow. It's gone!' said Nicky, very crossly.

'Don't worry,' laughed Mummy. 'It'll be back soon. Just wait for the sun to come out from behind that cloud.' They waited, and Mummy was right. A few seconds later, out popped the sun, and there was Nicky's shadow, nice and neat and black, right beside him. Nicky was pleased and zoomed off to the next corner, where he waited for Mummy to catch up.

'My shadow does everything the same as me,' he said.

'Yes, it's just like you,' agreed Mummy. 'It has even got your curly hair, look!'

Nicky nodded. 'Mmmm, we're both just the same.'

They did all the shopping quite quickly and then set off for home again. Mummy had a lot to carry, so she walked more slowly now. Nicky was practising hop-scotch along the pavement and thinking to himself.

Slap! Flip-flap! Slap! Flip-flap went his trainers, as he hopped and jumped along.

'Mummy?'

'Yes, Nicky.'

'Mummy, my shadow is just like me, but is there another *boy* like me?'

'Well, I don't know,' said Mummy. 'I expect there is another little boy somewhere who *looks* just like you, but he wouldn't be exactly the same. He would be different inside. He would like different games and talk a different way. No two people are *exactly* the same.'

Slap! Flip-flap! Slap! Flip-flap! Nicky was still thinking hard. 'Mummy, why did God make us all different?'

Mummy stopped and put down her shopping bags to rest her arms. 'Hmm, well maybe he thought it would be more interesting that way. It would be boring to be all the same. Being a bit different makes us all special.'

'Am I special?' asked Nicky.

'Oh, yes. Daddy and I think you're very special,' smiled Mummy, 'and God thinks you're very, *very* special.'

Nicky stopped hopping and nodded to himself, and then he smiled at Mummy. 'My shadow's special to me, too! . . . Can I have a lolly?' And he hopped all the way back to the crossing, without changing feet once.

Going swimming

It was Saturday, and Nicky and big brother Martin were going swimming with Mummy and Daddy.

'OK, boys,' said Daddy, 'let's just check that we've got everything we need before we go. Towels?'

'Yes!' shouted Nicky and Martin together.

'Trunks?'

'Yeees!'

'Armbands, Nicky?'

'Er . . . yes!'

'Goggles, Martin?'

'Of *course!*'

'Good. Now we're ready. Let's go.'

Nicky was looking worried. 'Mummy, what about our something-to-eat?'

Mummy held up some bags of crisps. 'All here, safe and sound.'

Now they really were ready and so off they went. It was a cold, blustery sort of day with leaves and sweet papers blowing about, and it was even trying to rain a bit. They hurried along, and Nicky and Martin galloped ahead, biffing each other with their swimming bags.

It didn't take long to reach the sports centre,

and in through the big glass doors they went. A puff of warm air, smelling of the swimming-pool, met them.

'Mmmm, it's nice and warm in here,' said Mummy, as she unbuttoned her jacket. 'I was beginning to wish that I'd stayed at home!'

While Daddy bought their tickets, Nicky pushed the buttons on the big vending machine that stood by the wall. He gazed longingly at the bars of chocolate and bags of sweets behind the glass.

'You've got to put money in first,' said Martin.

'I *know*,' Nicky replied, but he pushed another button, just in case.

'Come on, you two,' called Mummy, and they hurried off to get changed. Nicky went with Mummy because he still had trouble with buttons and things, especially when he was in a hurry.

'Quickly, Mummy!' he squeaked. 'We've *got* to be first!'

They hurried, but Daddy and Martin were quicker. 'Beat you!' Martin shouted.

'Don't care,' said Nicky. 'Armbands Mummy, armbands pleeease!' and he hopped up and down with impatience.

'Well, stop jigging and I'll be able to do them much faster!' Mummy laughed. She blew them up nice and fat, and at last Nicky was ready and slithering into the water.

'Oooh, nice!' he laughed, as he ducked his shoulders under.

'Not bad,' said Mummy, coming very slowly down the steps.

Daddy and Martin were off to the deeper water, to practise diving and swimming under water.

Nicky preferred to stay on *top* of the water. He could almost swim, but he still liked to wear his armbands, just in case. He really wanted to be able to swim and dive like Martin, and sometimes he felt quite cross when he thought about this, but he usually cheered up in the water because there were still a lot of things he could do.

'Look, Mummy, I'm being a mixer!' he shouted, as he wooshed his arms back and forward, turning the blue water to white froth. 'I'm making a milk-shake!' Next he blew bubbles and then he jumped up and down, seeing how far out of the water he could go.

'Right, Nicky,' said Mummy. 'Let's do a width of the pool without stopping and then we'll try without your armbands.'

Away they went, Nicky paddling furiously and Mummy swimming alongside, encouraging him. He managed very well and felt extremely pleased with himself, but he still didn't want to take off his armbands.

'I'm *sure* you could do it,' said Mummy and she went off across the pool again for a proper swim while Nicky practised floating on his back and looking at his toes.

Presently he looked up and saw his friend 'Lucy-down-the-road' sitting on the side of the pool. Lucy lived near Nicky. They often played together.

'Lucy!' he called, and he bobbed across the pool towards her. Lucy's mummy was already in the pool holding their baby gently in the water. He was chuckling and splashing, but Lucy didn't look very happy at all.

'Come on, Lucy,' said Nicky. 'It's nice and warm in here. Come and play paddle steamers!' Lucy shook her head and flicked one toe in the water.

'In you get, Lucy,' said her mummy. 'You'll be all right.' Lucy still didn't move. 'We've forgotten her armbands, and I can't hold on to her with little Sam to look after,' her mummy explained. Nicky's mummy came up.

'We'll give you a tow, Lucy. Come on, we'll look after you.' And at last, Lucy agreed to get into the water. Nicky and Mummy held her hands and she felt quite safe. Soon they were all laughing and splashing, as happy as could be.

'Shall we race across the pool now?' suggested Mummy after a while.

'Yeees!' yelled Nicky.

'No,' said Lucy, in a little voice. 'I can't do that without my armbands,' and she looked as though she might start crying. What could they do? Nicky looked at Mummy and Mummy looked at Nicky. Her eyebrows said, 'Well, how about it, then?' Nicky thought for a minute. Would he? Wouldn't he? Then very quickly before he could change his mind, he slipped off his armbands and held them out to Lucy.

'Here you are. I don't really need them now,' he said gruffly. Mummy gave him a special smile as she helped Lucy into the armbands.

'Now, are you ready . . . steady . . . Go!' and away they went. The water foamed and frothed as Nicky and Lucy raced for the other side. Mummy wasn't sure who had come first, because of all the splashing, but Nicky didn't mind because he and

Lucy were good friends and now he could really SWIM!

'Well *done*, Nicky,' said Mummy.

'I only put my feet down twice,' Nicky said.

When Daddy and Martin came back Nicky showed them how he could swim, and they said he was very clever. After that Martin, Nicky and Lucy played together in the shallow water and had lots of races. Then it was time to get out and go home, so Nicky said that Lucy could keep his armbands until she had finished. 'Bye, Lucy!' he called. Lucy smiled happily and waved.

'Goodbye, Nicky,' said Lucy's mummy, 'and thank you *very* much for cheering up Lucy.'

When Nicky and Mummy came out of the changing room Daddy and Martin were first again, but Nicky didn't mind this time. Mummy handed Martin and Daddy their crisps, and they hurried off to the shops to get something for Martin's bike.

'Can I have my crisps now, Mummy?' asked Nicky.

'Half a mo, Nicky.' Mummy was poking around in her purse. 'Ah, here we are,' she said, and she handed Nicky some money. 'I think you deserve something special today,' she said and they walked over to the vending machine.

On the way home Nicky was very quiet – he was busy eating his chocolate bar! When it was almost gone he said, 'Mummy, did I get this because I can swim now?'

'Yes, partly,' said Mummy, 'but also because you were a kind boy to Lucy.'

'Lucy was sad, wasn't she? I didn't like it when she was sad – she wouldn't play with me . . . she

19

was happy when I gave her my armbands!'

'Yes. Being kind is a really good way to make people happy . . . and it makes *you* happy too.'

Nicky nodded, but he didn't say anything because his cheeks were full with the last piece of his special chocolate bar.

Nuts

One Saturday Nicky and big brother Martin were playing in the park with Daddy. Although the sun was shining and the sky was very blue, it was quite cold and they were all running about to keep warm. Martin had brought his football and he and Daddy were practising dribbling and passing to each other. Nicky was joining in too, but he still wasn't very good at kicking and the ball never seemed to do what he wanted.

After a while Nicky was tired of football and he started to kick at the fallen leaves that were lying all over the grass and paths. It had been very windy during the night and nearly every leaf had been blown off the twigs and branches of the trees. They were standing, all cold and bare-looking, but the ground was a mass of yellow and brown and red patches, like one of the splash paintings Nicky had done at Playgroup. The leaves made a lovely pattering, swishing sound as he scuffled his feet through them.

Nicky swished his way along the path, keeping one eye on Daddy and Martin who were still kicking the ball about on the grass. Suddenly, just ahead of him, the path became clean and tidy, with only one or two dark brown leaves dancing across, all alone. The rest of the leaves were heaped up in a big pile, under a tall tree beside the path. It was a very big pile . . . a very inviting pile. 'Come on,' it seemed to be saying. 'Here I am, just sitting here doing nothing, waiting for someone to play with.'

'Wheee. . . . !' Nicky ran, jumped as high as he could, and landed – pfluff! – right in the middle of the big pile. He bounced and scuffled in the leaves. He threw armfuls into the air and watched them patter down around him. He kicked and he jumped. All at once, there was a loud voice. 'Oi!' it shouted. 'Get off my leaves!' Nicky stopped and looked up at the tree. Did trees talk? Had this big tree just shouted at him? Then he heard a sound behind him, and there was a Park man in blue overalls, with a twiggy broom and a wheelbarrow, looking rather cross.

'Come on. Off there,' he said. 'I've just spent the last hour making that pile and *now* look at it!'

Nicky scrambled out and looked. Yes, it was a very scattered, flat pile now. Not much of a pile at all really. 'Sorry,' he said, in a little voice.

Daddy and Martin came puffing up, and Daddy said sorry to the man too. Then the man smiled. 'It's OK. No hard feelings, eh?' So they all helped the man make the pile again, and soon the path was tidy once more.

'Right, Nicky,' said Daddy, 'I think we'd better go to the play area now.'

They had a lovely time swinging and sliding and climbing. While Nicky was crawling through the pipe tunnel he heard Martin shout. 'Hey! Look over there. It's a squirrel!' Nicky popped out at

the end of the pipe and there were Daddy and Martin, standing very still by the fence.

'Shhh,' said Daddy as Nicky ran to join them, 'look, there he is.'

For a moment Nicky couldn't see where Daddy was pointing, and then, not far away, he saw a little grey squirrel with a long bushy tail come bounding across the grass. 'He's got something in his mouth,' whispered Nicky.

'I bet it's a nut,' said Martin quietly, 'squirrels like nuts.' The squirrel stopped and began to scrabble in the grass with his front paws. Then he popped the nut into the hole he'd made, and patted the earth and grass down on top.

'What's he doing?' asked Nicky.

'I think he's burying some nuts, ready for the winter,' Daddy replied.

'Yes, he'll need those when it's cold and there's no food around,' Martin explained. Martin knew a lot of things like that.

'But how will he remember where he's put the nuts?' asked Nicky, looking worried.

'I don't really know *how* he remembers,' said Daddy, 'but he *does*. It's the way God made him. God knows the squirrel can't go shopping for food like we can and he doesn't want him to go hungry in the winter when there are no more berries and nuts on the trees.' Nicky thought that this was very clever. They watched the squirrel a bit longer and then a dog barked loudly nearby, and with a flip of his tail, the squirrel whisked up the nearest tree trunk and disappeared.

'Come on,' said Daddy. 'Time for lunch, boys.' And they hurried off home.

'I'm hungry! When's lunch?' shouted Martin and Nicky as they burst in at the back door. Mummy was busy with saucepans and the table was laid.

'It won't be long,' she said. 'What have you been doing?'

So Martin told her about Nicky and the leaves, and Nicky told her about the squirrel.

'I'm glad *we* don't have to bury our food for the winter,' said Nicky, as they all sat down at the table.

Mummy nodded. 'I'd *much* rather go shopping every week instead of having to dig in the garden each time we needed something to eat.'

Martin made a face. 'Buried baked beans, yuk!' and they all laughed.

'We need to thank God for giving us shops full of food to eat,' said Daddy. 'In some countries people don't have shops like us.'

'. . . . or enough food either,' added Martin.

Then Daddy asked, 'Whose turn is it to say Thank you?'

It was Nicky's. He shut his eyes and thought for a moment. Then he said, 'Thank you, God for helping the squirrel find his nuts in the winter . . . and thank you for always giving us nice food *every day*. Amen!'

Nicky and the fireman's helmet

'We're going to Playgroup, to Playgroup, to Playgroup!' sang Nicky as he skipped along the road with Mummy. Nicky had been at Playgroup since he was three and now he was nearly five, so he was one of the big children. He loved Playgroup mornings because his special friends, Edward and Charlene were there. He also liked it because big brother Martin *wasn't* there, bossing him about. At Playgroup there were lots of things to do, like painting and dough, and sandtray, and Home Corner. Now and again there were special extras like cooking, or a visit to a farm. Nicky was always very impatient to get there on Playgroup mornings.

'Come on, Mummy, hurry *up!*' he begged as Mummy stopped to look in a shoe shop window.

Mummy laughed. 'I think I'd better borrow Martin's roller skates next time and you can push me along really fast.'

'Hello there, Nicky,' said Betty as Nicky and Mummy came through the door and into the hall where the Playgroup met. Betty was the Playgroup leader, and she and her four helpers looked after the children all morning. Nicky thought Betty was lovely. She had very long hair and huge round spectacles, and she wore the brightest clothes that he had ever seen.

Today Betty was wearing a pink track-suit and pink and white trainers. Nicky didn't usually like pink because Martin said it was a girl's colour, but Betty looked *so* nice he couldn't help liking it. 'You look like candy floss!' he said to Betty.

She chuckled, 'Well, don't try eating me, will you? I may *look* like candy floss, but I'm sure I wouldn't *taste* like it!'

Mummy said goodbye and Nicky settled down on a little chair in the circle round Betty's big chair. He grinned at Edward who was already there. 'I got new shoes, look!' said Edward, and he stuck his feet straight out in front so Nicky could see. They were blue shoes with red laces, and very clean and new underneath.

'My shoes are old,' said Nicky and he waggled his feet up and down. Edward laughed and then they both waggled their feet so hard that they fell off their chairs.

'All right, you two,' laughed Betty. 'Back on your chairs; it's time for register.'

After Betty had called out all the names, everyone went off to play. Nicky and Edward made a motorway in the sand tray and brummmmed the little cars along it. Then they went off to the Home Corner. Charlene was already there with another little girl called Kirsty.

They were busy putting on dressing-up clothes and posing in front of the big mirror, admiring themselves.

'I'm a queen,' announced Charlene, as she wobbled about in long orange dress and golden shoes with spindly heels.

Nicky started to rummage through the hat box, then he suddenly noticed Kirsty. She had a long piece of net curtain round her head and a funny black hat perched on top.

'I'm a bride,' she said and twirled round to show Charlene.

Nicky stared at Kirsty's hat. 'That's the fireman's helmet,' he said in disgust. 'Brides don't wear helmets!' and he grabbed if off her head.

'No!' shouted Kirsty. 'Gimme my hat!'

'Yes, you give her that hat,' said Charlene, looking very fierce.

'Me and Edward are firemen and *we* need it, don't we?' said Nicky. Edward, who was standing safely behind Nicky, nodded bravely at the girls. Charlene snatched at the helmet and tripped over her long skirt. Thump! Down she fell.

'You give us that hat, Nicky,' she began to shout.

Kirsty was crying now. 'You bad, bad boy,' she sobbed. 'Give me my haaat!'

Suddenly Betty was there, with Jo, one of her helpers. 'What's going on here?' she asked. The girls were crying and shouting both at the same time, and Nicky stood holding the helmet, with his mouth all squeezed up tight and his forehead crinkly. Betty untangled Charlene and stood her up while Jo wiped Kirsty's eyes. 'Who had the helmet first?' asked Betty.

'She did!' said both girls together. 'I was being a bride,' added Kirsty in a little sad voice.

'But it's a fireman's helmet,' said Nicky in desperation. '*Brides* don't wear helmets!'

Edward nodded hard behind Nicky. For a moment it seemed as though Betty and Jo thought something was funny, but then Betty said in a serious voice, 'Well, Nicky, you and Edward may be right about brides not wearing helmets, but you were wrong to try and take it. We have only one helmet and it belongs to everyone, so we need to share it. I'm sure the girls will let you have a turn with it in a while, *won't* you?' and she looked at Charlene and Kirsty over her glasses. They nodded cheerfully.

Nicky hung his head and squeezed his mouth even tighter. 'Come on, now,' said Betty. 'Say sorry and then we'll find something for you two to do.'

'Sorry,' muttered Nicky in a gruff voice.

'Pardon?' said Betty.

'SORRY!'

'That's better. Now how about you and Edward helping me with this new floor puzzle?' Soon the boys were so busy they forgot all about the helmet. Before long it was milk and biscuits time, and then there was a story. Finally they all played 'The farmer's in the dell' and Betty chose Nicky to be the farmer, and he chose Charlene to be his wife, and they were friends again.

Nicky was rather quiet on the way home from Playgroup. At lunch-time Mummy asked, 'Did you enjoy Playgroup today?'

'Mmmm,' Nicky nodded, with a mouth full of honey sandwich, 'but Charlene and Kirsty were silly.' And he told Mummy about the fireman's helmet.

'Betty was right you know,' said Mummy, when

he'd finished explaining. 'You shouldn't have taken it off Kirsty. You've got to share.' Nicky looked down at his plate and kept eating.

'Jesus wants us to love other people, doesn't he?' reminded Mummy. 'Being kind and sharing is a way of loving people.'

'Even when they're silly?' asked Nicky. Mummy nodded.

Nicky sighed. It all seemed a bit hard. He knew he'd been wrong to snatch the helmet and he knew it was good to share, and he had felt unhappy when Kirsty cried, but he'd *needed* that helmet. He thought hard while he finished his sandwiches.

'Mummy, if I found another hat for Kirsty then it'd be all right to have the helmet, wouldn't it?'

Mummy smiled.

'That would be a good idea,' she said.

Nicky bounced up and down in his chair. 'Then Kirsty and Charlene would be happy . . . and me an' Edward would be happy . . . and Jesus would be happy, too!'

Next Playgroup morning Nicky burst into the hall carrying a big plastic bag. In it was a straw hat with a wide, floppy brim. It had ribbons around it and a fat pink rose at the back. 'Oh my!!' exclaimed Betty when she saw it. 'How lovely.'

'It's for the girls, so we can have the helmet,' explained Nicky.

Betty looked at Nicky's Mummy. 'Are you *sure*? It's such a pretty hat.'

Mummy laughed. 'I haven't worn it for years, and anyway, I think you need it more than I do.'

Edward arrived and Nicky went to meet him, wearing the helmet.

'Come on, Edward. Let's put out the fire.'

'Just a minute, young man,' called Betty. 'Come and say goodbye to your mum.' Nicky hurried back for a hug and a kiss. 'Bye, Nicky,' said Mummy. 'Have fun, and don't forget to. . . .

'. . . . Share!' replied fireman Nicky, and with a hop and a skip he was off again to put out the fire.

'Bee-bah, bee-bah, bee-bah, bee-bah..!'

The listening day

'Pyow! Pyow! I got you!'

'No you didn't. . . . here I come. . . . nyaaow, nyaaow, NYAAOW! Got you!' Nicky and his friend, Edward, were having a wonderful time in Nicky's back garden one sunny afternoon.

Edward had come back for lunch after Playgroup, and now they were playing a really exciting game. They were dashing and shouting all over the garden; leaping over flower-beds, dodging behind the shed, rolling across the grass, and making a tremendous NOISE. Nicky had got Edward for the third time, and Edward had just caught Nicky and was sitting on his chest when Mummy came out of the house.

'Let's have a little bit less noise, shall we?' she suggested. 'The neighbours will think we've got twenty boys in here, not just two of you!'

'But Mummy. . . .'

'. . . . and look at you, your faces are bright red. It's *far* too hot to be running about like that.'

Nicky and Edward sat down on the back doorstep, puffing and panting. They really did feel quite hot and tired.

'But what *can* we do?' asked Nicky.

'Sit there while I fetch you a drink, and then I think I've got an idea.'

When Mummy came back and they were having their drinks, she told them her idea. 'This is a good game to play when you're tired and your voices need a rest. We're all going to sit very quiet and still for one minute and use our *ears*. We're going to listen very hard to see what we can hear. There are lots of different sounds all around us, all the time, but the trouble is we often make so much noise ourselves that we don't hear them. Are you ready?' Mummy looked at her watch and the boys sat quietly. A few seconds passed.

'Mummy. . . .'

'Shhh!'

Nicky sighed. A minute is a long time when you're sitting still *and* being quiet, but at last it was over.

'Right then,' said Mummy. 'What did you hear?'

There was a pause and then Edward said, 'I heard a car.'

'So did I, and a lorry.'

'Anything else?' Mummy asked. The boys shook their heads. 'Dear me, you aren't very good at listening, are you? Let's try again, and this time we'll make a list. Some sounds are very quiet or far-away, so you'll need to listen carefully or you may miss them. Shutting your eyes might help, too.' This time the boys tried really hard and, to their surprise they *did* hear more things. Here are some of the sounds they heard. Do you know what they were?

'Tweet-tweet, twit-twit-twit, tweet.'

'Wuff, wuff.'

'Clack, clack, clack, clack.'

'Brrummm, brrrrummmmm.'

'Bzzzzzz. . . .'

Mummy drew a little picture of each sound on a big piece of paper, as the boys told her. There was a bird, a dog, a pair of shoes for the footsteps, a car and a lorry, and a thing that might have been a bee or a fly, but they weren't sure because they had all had their eyes shut!

'Well, that's quite a list,' said Mummy, 'but I'm sure we'll hear more. We'll stop and have another listen in a little while.'

So the boys went off to play again, a little bit quieter than before, and Mummy went back indoors.

For the rest of the afternoon, every now and then, Mummy would stop whatever she was doing and get the boys to sit down and listen again. The picture list grew and grew and, by the time Edward's Mummy came to collect him, they'd almost filled the paper. Among other sounds they heard were voices from the street, the next door neighbour's lawn mower, the washing machine in Nicky's house, someone's radio playing music, the chimes of the ice cream van, and a power-saw trimming branches from a tree in the next street.

When big brother Martin came home from school, he joined the listening game and they added an aeroplane, a motor bike, and the siren of a fire-engine. By the time Daddy got in they'd turned the paper over and begun to fill the other side.

'Goodness!' laughed Daddy, as he looked at the list. 'I didn't know we lived in such a noisy place!'

'You should have heard it *before* we started the

game,' said Mummy.

At bedtime Nicky had almost filled the second side of the paper. When he was tucked up in bed he added two more sounds – his little clock and the rain that had just begun to fall. 'Pit-pat' it went, and 'swooooosh' went the cars along the wet road.

Mummy came up to say goodnight and sat and looked at the picture list with Nicky. 'We really heard a lot of things today, didn't we?' Nicky nodded.

'I liked our listening day,' he said. 'Ears are very useful things, aren't they?'

'Yes,' agreed Mummy. 'We need to thank God that our ears work so well. Some people's ears don't, you know.'

'Mmm,' said Nicky. 'Like Grandad! He says "What's that?" a lot, doesn't he?'

'He won't, now he's got a hearing-aid,' said Mummy.

'That's a thing that goes behind your ear, isn't it?' said Nicky sleepily. 'Marie at Playgroup has one of those.'

'You see, even children sometimes don't hear very well.'

'I wonder if Grandad could make a list like ours now he can hear properly?' Nicky murmured. 'I'm glad my ears work OK.'

'Night-night,' said Mummy. Nicky lay quietly, listening to the night-time sounds – the rain pit-patting and the cars swooshing and his little clock ticking. 'Thank you, God that I can hear,' he thought. Pit-pat, pat, pit, pat-pit-pit. . . . swoosh, tick-tick-tick-tick-tick, pit-pat, pit . . . pat . . .

pit . . . swoosh . . . tick-tick . . . pit . . . pat . . .
tick-tick . . . pit . . . pat . . . on and on, but
Nicky didn't hear anything more because he was
fast asleep.

Martin goes to hospital

One day, after Playgroup, Nicky was surprised to find Grannie at the door to collect him. 'Where's Mummy?' he asked, as he struggled into his anorak.

'Hold still a minute and put that arm in there. . . . she's had to take Martin to the hospital. Your silly brother tried to bang a hole in the school playground with his head. He was playing football, and he tripped over and hit his head. His teacher thought the doctor should look at it, just to make sure he's all right.'

Nicky was interested. 'Was there any blood?'

Grannie chuckled. 'No! Only a big blue bump and a headache!'

'Did they go in an ambulance – with a flashing light?'

'Goodness me, no! One of the teachers took them in her car.'

'Oh,' said Nicky, rather disappointed. 'What's for lunch?'

Grannie gave Nicky his lunch and then he played busily all afternoon. The phone rang, and Grannie talked for a while. 'Yes . . . no. . . . all right. . . . no, don't worry, Nicky's fine. . . .' Afterwards she said, 'That was Mummy. The doctor took an X-ray picture of Martin's head and he's all right, but he wants him to stay in hospital tonight, just to rest it. Mummy's going to stay with him, to keep him company.'

'What about me?' asked Nicky.

'Well, Daddy will be home soon, and I'll stay with you until then. Come on now and we'll go and find the things Mummy and Martin will need tonight.' So Nicky and Grannie bustled about, looking for things like tooth brushes, pyjamas and story books. Then they packed them all into a bag and when Daddy came home he was able to take it over to the hospital. When he got back Grannie said goodbye and went off to her house.

'Now for something to eat!' said Daddy. 'Mummy's given me a list of things for tea,' and he began to poke about in the fridge and cupboards, while Nicky helped to lay the table. What a meal they had! It wasn't quite like Mummy made, but it was very interesting. They had beef burgers and beans with very thick slices of bread, because Daddy said that was quicker than potatoes. Daddy let Nicky put tomato sauce on his beans, which Mummy never did.

Then they had lots of ice cream, with squirty chocolate topping, and a whole Swiss roll that Daddy found in a cake tin. Afterwards they both felt *very* full!

'Time for bed, Nicky,' said Daddy. It wasn't until he was in bed that Nicky began to feel rather sad. It was too quiet. There was no Martin on the top bunk, and no Mummy to come and kiss him goodnight. Daddy noticed that Nicky wasn't very

happy. 'What's the matter, mate?' he asked.

'I want Mummy,' said Nicky in a shaky voice, and he began to cry.

'I know how you feel,' said Daddy putting an arm around Nicky, 'but Martin needs Mummy tonight. He's got a sore head and he might be unhappy if Mummy didn't stay with him.'

'But I don't like it here by myself,' snuffled Nicky. 'I'm *lonely!*'

'But you're not alone,' said Daddy. 'I'm here, and of course, God's with you. He's always with us, even when we're asleep. God never sleeps.'

'Why not?'

'Well, because he's God, and he doesn't need to.'

'What about Mummy and Martin?'

'He's with them, too.'

'He can't be *there* and *here*, that's too difficult!'

'It would be for us, but God is so wonderful, he can do it. Nothing's too difficult for him.'

Nicky had a lot to think about as he went off to sleep that night. He and Daddy had asked God to look after Mummy and Martin in hospital, and to make Martin's head better soon. Now Daddy was lying on Martin's top bunk, keeping Nicky company until he went to sleep. 'I'm not lonely because Daddy's here, and even if he goes to sleep, God will still be awake. . . .' he thought sleepily.

Next morning as they were eating their breakfast, the phone rang and it was Mummy saying, 'Come and fetch us. We can come home!' So, in no time at all, they were off to the hospital.

When Daddy and Nicky arrived they found Mummy and Martin looking the same as they always did. Nicky was so pleased to see them, but especially Mummy. She hugged him and explained that Martin's head was better now, and that the doctor had said he could go back to school, so long as he didn't go bashing the playground again. Then she gave a huge yawn and Daddy said, 'Hmmm, I think we'd better take Mummy home and put her to bed. She looks very sleepy.'

Mummy laughed, 'I *could* do with a nap. Hospitals are noisy places at night, and I didn't sleep very much.'

'God doesn't sleep *at all*,' said Nicky, as they walked together to the car park. 'He doesn't need to . . . and do you know, he was here with you and Martin *and* with me and Daddy . . . all night, even when we were asleep . . . only he can do it, though, because he's God. Nothing's too difficult for God!'

Nicky and the flowers

One morning Nicky woke up, and after he had done a big stretch, he curled up again under his quilt and looked at his little clock on the chest of drawers. Daddy had shown him where the hands must be for getting-up-time: 'long hand straight up, short hand on seven.' Nicky could see that the short hand was in the right place, but the long hand still had a little way to go, so he knew he must wait a bit longer.

He rolled over and stared at the curtains that covered the bedroom window. They were special ones that Mummy had made when Nicky and big brother Martin had got their new bunk beds. With just his eyes peeping out from under his quilt Nicky could see the rows of colourful animals prancing and dancing across a jungly-green background. What a strange collection of animals they were too! Fat blue hippos, pink elephants, green and orange crocodiles, yellow lions and a few that Nicky didn't know and even Daddy wasn't sure about. Nicky liked their stripes and spots, and the way the folds in the curtains made the animals into even stranger shapes; like funny monsters. Of course, Nicky knew that *real* elephants and lions were greys and browns and colours like that, because he'd seen pictures of them in books and on television. He liked the funny 'pretend' animals though, because they looked bright and friendly. Nicky lay and wondered what they were doing. Perhaps they were having a race, or maybe it was a sort of procession, like a carnival? He started to make up a story about the hippo and the elephant going for a walk. They had only got as far as meeting Mr Lion and Mr Lion was just saying, 'Good morning Fat Hippo and Pink Elephant . . .' when Nicky felt the bed wobble and there was a thump as Martin jumped down from his top bunk.

Today was one of the days when Nicky had no Playgroup so after Martin had gone off to school, Nicky had to find something to do. First he helped Mummy put the breakfast toast crusts out for the birds, and then he pottered about in the garden on his bike. It was too early for his morning television so he wondered what to do next. Then he decided to have a dig in his special muddy patch beside the shed, because he hadn't been there for a while.

He fetched a spade from the sandpit and skipped down the garden but when he reached the place where his muddy patch used to be, it was gone! All the nice brown mud was covered in little green plants and some of them even had bright orange flowers coming out of them. At first Nicky thought he was going to be cross about his muddy patch, but then he found that he was very interested.

He crouched down for a closer look and peered at the fat, green leaves. Then he poked a flower with his finger. A big striped bee seemed very interested too. It sat on the petals of a flower and made it bounce up and down.

Mummy came into the garden with the washing basket. 'Mummy, come and see!' shouted Nicky, 'Something's growing on my mud!'

'Well,' said Mummy, 'Do you know what? I think those are the marigold seeds we planted in the spring. I'd forgotten about them. They're lovely!'

Nicky had forgotten about the seeds too, but he was very pleased to see the flowers now. For the rest of the day he kept popping up the garden to check on them, and of course, when Martin and Daddy came home they had to see them too. 'Fancy that!' said Daddy, after he had admired them. 'I'd never have thought anything would grow in your mud-hole, Nicky. Wasn't it wonderful of God not to forget those seeds you planted? He's made them grow into lovely flowers and given us all a surprise.'

That evening at bed-time, Nicky proudly carried a jam jar upstairs. In it were five bright orange marigold flowers. Mummy had helped him cut them carefully with the kitchen scissors. He put them on the chest of drawers next to the clock, so that he could see them from his bed. When he was tucked in, Nicky looked at the lovely bright flowers and then at the cheerful animals on the curtains and he smiled to himself.

'What are you thinking about?' asked Daddy, who had come to say goodnight.

'God must be very busy making all the flowers and animals,' said Nicky. 'And clever too – giving them all the right colours.'

'Yes,' agreed Daddy. 'Pink and blue and yellow

are all right for 'pretend' animals, but not for real ones. I'm glad he made them nice, sensible colours, aren't you?'

Nicky yawned and said, 'I'm glad he made our flowers very *bright*. . . . and that he didn't forget about the seeds, like we did!'

Lost and found

'Bing-bong,' the door-bell rang, just after Nicky and Mummy had come home from Playgroup. Mummy was busy stirring their lunch-time soup.

'See who it is and then come and tell me,' she said. Nicky hurried to peer through the glass in the door.

'Mummy! It's Grannie!' he called.

'Oh, well, I think we can let her in!' laughed Mummy.

'Would you like some lunch, Mum?' she asked, as Grannie came into the kitchen. 'We're just going to have ours.' Grannie shook her head, and Nicky saw that she was not her usual smiley self.

'No thanks, love,' she sighed. 'I don't feel like eating. You see, I've lost my purse, and I'm very worried.'

Mummy looked worried too, and Nicky could see that this was a very serious matter. 'Tell us what happened,' said Mummy.

'Well, I went to the Post Office yesterday morning, to collect my pension. I had my purse then because I put my pension money in it. Then I did my shopping, and on my way home I visited my friend, Mrs White. I didn't know my purse was lost until I went to pay the milkman this morning.'

'Where have you looked for it?' Mummy asked.

'*Everywhere!*' replied Grannie sadly. 'All round the house, along the roads, in the shops, and even around Mrs White's house. I just can't think where it's gone.' Poor Grannie. She looked so worried.

'Well, we'll all sit down and have a think,' said Mummy. So Nicky and Mummy had their soup and toast, and Grannie drank a cup of coffee.

'Have you lost *all* your money?' asked Nicky as he ate.

'No, my love, not *all* of it, but quite a lot. It's *so* annoying. I hate losing things. I'm a silly Grannie, aren't I?'

'Nonsense,' said Mummy firmly. 'We all lose things sometimes. Now, I wonder what we ought to do first?'

'I know,' said Nicky, as he chased the last piece of mushroom round his soup bowl. 'We should tell Jesus.' Grannie and Mummy looked at Nicky and then at each other.

'He's right y'know,' said Grannie with a laugh that was almost like her usual one. 'I've been so busy worrying and searching I forgot to tell Jesus my problem!'

So straight away they told Jesus about the lost purse and how Grannie was feeling sad and worried and how she didn't know what to do next. Afterwards Grannie looked a lot happier, and Mummy said, 'Now, let's start back at the beginning and do a proper search, all the way from the Post Office to your house.'

And that's just what they did. They started at the Post Office, where Grannie had gone first, and they asked in every shop that Grannie had visited the day before. They went into the butcher's shop, the fruit and vegetable shop, the dry-cleaner's, the newsagent's and the grocer's, but no, no one had seen Grannie's purse.

'Are you *sure* we've been to all the shops you went into yesterday?' asked Mummy. They were all feeling tired and fed-up.

'Yes,' said Grannie. 'I didn't go anywhere else. . . . except . . . wait a minute, I forgot the baker's! I popped in there last of all to get Mrs White's bread order. How stupid of me to forget!' So they all hurried along to the baker's shop. This was Nicky's favourite shop because it was always warm and smelled so nice and there were so many lovely things to look at in the window.

'I'm looking for a purse,' Grannie told the lady behind the counter. 'A big brown purse, with a gold clip. I lost it yesterday.'

The lady smiled and said, 'Just a minute.' She disappeared down behind the counter and then bobbed up again like a big puppet at the Punch and Judy show. In her hand she held. . . . a big, brown purse. 'Is this it?' she asked brightly.

'It certainly *is!*' said Grannie. 'Well, what a relief. We've looked everywhere for this, haven't we, Nicky?'

The lady smiled. 'We found it in the corner when we swept the floor last night. You must have dropped it and it somehow got kicked over there where no one could see it. I'm glad you came. We were going to take it to the Police Station this evening.' Nicky and Mummy smiled as Grannie thanked the lady.

'Well now, I think we need to celebrate, don't you?' said Grannie to Mummy and Nicky. 'Let's all choose something to eat with our afternoon cup of tea.'

Nicky thought this was an excellent idea. Mummy and Grannie quickly chose an apple strudel and a macaroon, but Nicky took so long deciding that the shop lady had to serve some other customers while he made up his mind. He gazed at the trays of cream cakes, chocolate biscuits and iced buns, and at last he chose a jam doughnut.

Grannie and Mummy kept their cakes for later, but Mummy said, seeing as he hadn't had much lunch, Nicky could eat his doughnut on the way home. 'Is that good, Nicky?' asked Grannie as they walked along.

'Mmmm,' said Nicky through a jammy, sugary moustache.

'What do you say to Grannie?' Mummy whispered.

'Oh, thank you, Grannie,' said Nicky quickly.

'No, thank *you*, Nicky,' laughed Grannie. 'It was you who reminded me to tell Jesus about my lost purse.'

They were nearly home and Nicky had been very quiet, then he said thoughtfully, 'Actually, you should say thank you to Jesus as well.'

'I already *have*, my love,' replied Grannie, and she gave him a hug.

'It's a pity we can't give Jesus a thank you bun,' Nicky murmured, as he licked his fingers.

'Seeing us happy and hearing our thank yous is what Jesus really likes,' said Grannie. 'Isn't that right?' and she looked at Mummy.

'Yes, I'm sure that's the kind of thank you Jesus would want. Now come here, Nicky, and let me wipe your face. I think there's more "thank you bun" outside you than inside!'

The little accident

'Pass the cornflakes!'
  'More toast, Mummy!'
  'Pardon?'
  'Please, Mummy.'
  'Mind your elbows, Martin.'
Nicky and his family were having breakfast one morning in the school holidays. Nicky was pouring cereal and milk into his bowl and Mummy was slicing bread for the toaster. Martin was half-way through his second slice of toast, and Daddy was sitting next to the radio, with his ear pressed against it.

'Be quiet! I can't hear the cricket score,' he grumbled. Nicky tried to eat quietly but his cornflakes seemed extra scrunchy this particular morning. He and Martin looked at Daddy and then at each other.

Nicky scrunched again and they both giggled. Martin reached across the table for the honey jar and knocked Nicky's milk over.

'Oops! Sorry!'

'Oh *Martin*, I told you to mind those elbows!' said Mummy.

'It was only an accident,' said Martin.

'Mr Clumsy!' teased Nicky.

'I'm not!'

'Mr Clumsy! Mr Clumsy!'

'QUIET!' roared Daddy, and this time they were quiet. Breakfast was finished with no more accidents, and Daddy clicked off the radio.

'Where are you going?' Mummy asked as he went out the back door.

'Got to do the plugs on the car,' he muttered, and then he was gone. Mummy sighed.

'Right boys, and what are *you* doing?'

'Can I go to Simon's and swop football stickers?' asked Martin. 'His mum said I could.'

'All right, but don't be too long. We're going down to the river for a picnic when Dad's fixed the car.'

Nicky had plans too. He and his friend 'Lucy-down-the-road' had been busy the day before, digging for treasure in Nicky's muddy patch at the end of the garden. They had made quite a deep hole and found some interesting things like bones, and pieces of broken china. They had washed everything carefully in a bucket of water and put them in an old flower pot. Nicky couldn't wait to get to work again with his trowel and bucket. I might find *real* treasure today, he thought to himself.

He dug and dug and soon the hole was even bigger. His pile of bits and pieces had grown, too. There were some more bits of china, some with pretty patterns on, a big rusty bolt and a plastic car with no wheels. He was just wondering whether he'd stop digging and turn his hole into a pond when Mummy called from the back door.

He dropped the trowel and galloped up the garden for his drink and biscuits. Hard work made him hungry!

'When you've finished, ask Daddy if he'd like a cup of coffee,' said Mummy and Nicky nodded, his nose deep in his mug of orange.

He found Daddy still working on the car. The bonnet was up and he was bent right over, clinking and banging and puffing away inside the engine somewhere. Nicky liked to look inside when Daddy put up the bonnet. There were lots of black, oily bits and coiling wires and knobby screws and things. Nicky wished *he* could unscrew things with a spanner and have black fingers like Daddy. For a moment he forgot Mummy's message, as he gazed at the insides of the car.

'Can I help?' he asked.

'No,' said Daddy's voice from somewhere under the bonnet.

'What does this bit do?'

'Don't touch, it's dirty!' came Daddy's voice again.

Nicky looked at Daddy's toolbox, lying by his feet on the drive-way. There were all sizes of spanners and some big pliers and tins of loose screws and nuts and bolts. He picked up a screwdriver.

'Do you need this one yet?' he asked hopefully.

'Nick, I'm busy. Please go away,' Daddy's voice said firmly.

Nicky sighed and picked up the biggest spanner he could find. It was really big and really heavy.

I bet Edward couldn't lift this, he thought. Perhaps even Martin couldn't lift it. I can lift it 'cause I'm *very* strong. He held it above his head with both hands. 'I'm strong! See how strong I am!'

'*Nicky!*' Nicky jumped and the spanner flew out of his hands. 'KLUNK!' it hit the side of the car and then fell with a clank to the ground. Daddy came out from the car's insides. He was very angry. He took Nicky's arm and shook him and then he smacked him hard.

'How many times have I told you *not* to touch my tools?' he shouted. 'You could have dented the car or scratched the paint. You're a naughty boy!'

Nicky started to cry. 'But I wanted to help. It was just an accident,' he wailed.

Mummy heard the noise and came to see what was happening. Nicky was crying and crying.

'Keep that child out of the way or I'll never get this done,' Daddy growled, and he disappeared inside the car again.

Mummy took Nicky, still crying loudly, back into the house. He sat on her lap while she dried his eyes. 'Now, what have you been up to?' she asked.

Nicky explained what had happened. ' . . . and I only wanted to help,' he sniffed. 'It's not fair. It was only a little accident. Why's Daddy so grumpy today?'

'Well, said Mummy, 'Daddy's rather worried about something at his work. It's something very difficult that he's got to do. It'll be all right soon, when it's done.'

'But he *shouted*,' said Nicky, 'and you say I mustn't shout at Martin.'

'Yes, none of us should shout really, but I think that being worried is making Daddy grumpy.'

Nicky sniffed. 'I think I'll go and dig,' he said.

Later, when Nicky's hole was enormous and he'd decided it should definitely be a pond, Daddy came up the garden. 'That's a good hole, Nick,' he said. Nicky nodded.

'Have you found any treasure yet?' Nicky nodded again and pointed to the flowerpot.

'I found some bones,' he said. 'It could be a dinosaur.'

'Could be,' agreed Daddy, and he sat down on a big upturned flowerpot. 'I'm sorry I shouted at you. I shouldn't have been so cross, but I'm a bit worried about something.'

'Daddies don't get worried,' said Nicky.

'They do sometimes,' Daddy answered with a laugh. 'But I shouldn't have got so cross with you.'

'I didn't mean to bang the car,' said Nicky sadly.

'No, I know it was an accident but you *were* naughty to fiddle with my tools.' Nicky nodded. That was fair really, he thought.

'I think we should talk to God about what's happened,' said Daddy. So they told God about Daddy being worried and about how it had made him cross. Daddy said he was sorry for shouting at Nicky, and Nicky said he was sorry for getting in the way. Afterwards they were happy and felt good friends again.

Crash! Thud! That was Martin bursting in at the back gate. 'I'm home! Are we ready to go to the river?'

'Yes, the car's all done now,' said Daddy.

'Yippee! Come on, Nick. Let's get our wellies and fishing nets.'

Martin dashed indoors and Nicky and Daddy

followed him. 'When we get home again, would you like to help me wash the car?' Daddy asked.

'With the hose?' Nicky wanted to know.

'Yes!'

'And lots of soap and bubbles?'

'Certainly!'

Nicky gave a hop and a skip of pleasure and ran off to help Martin look for the fishing nets.

Grannie's special drink

'Ker-TISH-OOO!'

'Good gracious me, what was that?' asked Grannie, popping her head round the bedroom door.

'It's be,' said Nicky. 'I'b poorly. I'b dot a code.'

'Yes, you certainly have, you poor old thing,' agreed Grannie.

'Bubby says I can't do to Blaygroub because of by gerbs,' snuffled Nicky sadly.

'Quite right too,' laughed Grannie. 'No one else will want to share your sniffles!'

Nicky was sitting on the bedroom floor, nearly dressed and struggling to put on his socks. 'You've almost dressed yourself, you good boy,' said Grannie, smiling her twinkly smile. 'Are you having trouble with those socks?'

Nicky nodded, 'Stupid socks. They're all flippy-floppy ad they wote do od!'

'Come on then,' laughed Grannie, bending down to help. 'Let's sort you out. Now look, these poor socks aren't really silly, you know. This baggy bit here goes *under* your foot, for your heel to go in. You've put them on upside down!'

In no time at all Nicky's socks and slippers were

on. 'Now,' said Grannie, 'we'll go and wave goodbye to Mummy and then see what we can find to do.'

This morning Mummy had to go out and, because Nicky wasn't at Playgroup, Grannie had come to look after him. Grannie often came to visit Nicky and his big brother Martin, and they liked it when she did. Grannie was Mummy's mummy and she was always laughing. She always had time to read stories and sing songs, and sometimes she told them about the funny things Mummy and her brother had done when they were little. Nicky and Grannie went downstairs and waved from the front door till Mummy went around the corner.

'Right!' said Grannie, shutting the front door and looking at Nicky with her head on one side. 'What now? Is it going to be Hide and Seek or shall we have a story? Or maybe we could do another page in that new colouring book of yours?' Nicky hunched up his shoulders and shoved his hands into his pockets. He didn't feel like doing *anything*. His nose was stuffed-up and sneezy, his eyes were watering and he had a sort of scratchy bit in his throat. He sighed a great big sigh. Grannie was still looking at him with her head on one side and a twinkly look in her eyes.

'Oh, deary-me, this is serious,' she said. 'I can see we're going to need something special to cheer you up today. Come on!' and she bustled into the kitchen with Nicky trailing behind. 'Now, let's give your nose a good blow, and then I'm going to need your help with this job,' said Grannie as she filled the kettle and switched it on. Then she began to bang about in the cupboards looking for things.

'Where's your mug, Nicky? And where does Mummy keep the honey?' Nicky climbed up on a stool and unhooked his special mug from the rack, while Grannie rummaged in her shopping bag. 'Now, where did I put it? . . . I know I brought one . . . It's just as well I did my shopping on the way here . . . Ah, here we are!' and she held up a shiny fat lemon. 'Just the job! Are you ready?'

Nicky was beginning to be quite interested in what was going on, even though he felt so coldy. He climbed back up on to the stool and perched next to Grannie at the worktop. She had found Mummy's chopping board and a sharp knife, and was slicing the lemon right down the middle. 'I'll do this bit,' she chuckled. 'We don't want sore *fingers* as well as a sore throat! Now, it's your turn.' Grannie handed Nicky half the lemon and showed him how to press it down over the top of the lemon squeezer. It was hard work but Nicky kept pushing and pressing until the juice stopped coming out and the skin was all squishy. Then Grannie did the other half because his hands were tired and sticky.

'Let's have your mug now,' said Grannie. 'And one for me too.' She poured the lemon juice into the mugs. Then, while she fetched the hot kettle, Nicky found a teaspoon and fished out some lemon pips that had got into the juice by mistake.

'There!' said Grannie, as she poured hot water into the mugs. 'Now for the honey!' Nicky unscrewed the lid of the jar very carefully and stuck his spoon into the honey. 'That's right, a

nice big dollop!' laughed Grannie. Oh, and didn't it look lovely as he let it plop off the spoon and into the hot juice. Nicky did one for Grannie too, and then stirred and stirred until it was all mixed in. 'Ka-tink, ka-tink, ka-tink,' went the teaspoon inside each mug. Then Grannie put both mugs on a tray and they went into the sitting-room and sat and sipped together. Grannie's drink was lovely – all warm and sticky.

'Mmmmm,' said Nicky. 'This is dice.'

'Yes,' agreed Grannie, 'it's jolly good for colds and sore throats.'

'But *you* haven't dot a code!' Nicky pointed out.

'Oh, well maybe it will stop me catching one!' laughed Grannie.

After finishing his drink Nicky felt much better and he showed Grannie the Lego car he was making and they did four more pages in his new colouring book.

'Now, let's sing,' said Nicky.

'All right,' agreed Grannie, 'but *gently* so's not to hurt your throat.' So Nicky taught Grannie his new Playgroup songs and they both sang some of his Sunday school songs. 'I want to sing the Sunbeab one dow, Graddie,' said Nicky. When Grannie had taught him this one she had told him that it was one of Mummy's favourites, when she was little. So they sang, 'Jesus wants me for a sunbeam' and Nicky was really smiley and happy by the end of it. 'You're more like our little sunbeam now, Nicky,' said Grannie, and she gave him a hug.

'Jesus will love be now I'b a happy sudbeab, won't he Graddie?' asked Nicky.

Grannie laughed out loud. 'Oh, but he loves you *all* the time; even when you were a grumpy, coldy boy. He *knew* you didn't feel well,' and they gave each other another hug.

Suddenly there was a 'bing-bong' on the doorbell and Mummy was home.

'Well, Nicky, how's my poorly boy?' she asked as she hung up her jacket.

'Graddie gave be a special drink and I'b *much* better,' he grinned.

'This sounds very interesting,' said Mummy. 'Can I have a special drink too?'

They went into the kitchen. 'Sorry!' laughed Grannie. 'You'll have to buy another lemon!' and she pointed to the squished-up skins on the chopping board.

Mummy looked at the nearly-empty jar and the teaspoon lying in a sticky honey puddle. 'Looks like I'll have to buy some more honey, too!' and she and Grannie laughed together.

'Come on, Sunbeam,' said Grannie to Nicky. 'Let's make Mummy a nice cup of tea!'

The really bad day

Once, when Nicky was almost five, he had a really bad day. It started off badly and it went on being bad. First, his favourite sweater was in the wash and he was cross because he wanted to wear it to Playgroup.

Then his breakfast was all wrong. He said that his cornflakes were sharp and hurt his teeth, his toast was bendy, and the honey kept dripping off. After that, his milk was too cold, and then it was too hot. By this time he and Mummy were not very good friends, and she sent him off to play while she finished making big brother Martin's school sandwiches.

Nicky wandered upstairs and into their bedroom. Martin was there, getting his school clothes on. On the window sill, sitting on a sheet of newspaper, was a model car that Martin had nearly finished making. It had come in a box, in lots of tiny pieces, with a tube of special glue. Nicky thought it looked interesting and had wanted very much to help, but Martin had said he was too little. Nicky drifted over to the window sill and started to pick up the model.

'Hey, put that down, Nicky, the glue's still wet,'

said Martin.

'I'm just *looking* at it,' snapped Nicky, but he didn't put it down.

'Leave it alone, it's not a toy. You'll break it. . . . MUM!' Nicky put the car down quickly and scuttled out of the room.

Later on at Playgroup, things didn't go well either. To start with, Edward and Charlene, his special Playgroup friends, weren't there. Edward had a cough, and Charlene was on holiday. Nicky didn't settle to anything. All the activities seemed boring and he didn't want to play with anyone else. 'I don't know what's the matter with him today,' said Mummy when she collected him.

Betty, the Playgroup lady, laughed. 'He's just having one of those days! . . . I think he's ready for school, too!'

After lunch, which, to Mummy's relief, had no sharp bits and wasn't too hot or too cold, Nicky wandered back upstairs.

He was looking for his army jeep in the bottom of the wardrobe when Martin's model car caught his eye. Well now, he knew that he shouldn't touch it, and he knew it was very special to Martin, but he was feeling so grumpy that he *didn't care*. He picked up the car. It was a lovely one – a model rally car, and it had lots of extra bits on it: mirrors and a steering wheel, and tiny seat belts – all much better than his toy cars. Nicky brummed it very gently along the window sill. The wheels went round very nicely.

He brummed it a bit harder and let it go. It whizzed along the window sill beautifully. He brummed it again and wheee. . . . CRASH! it shot off sideways and fell to the floor. 'Oops!' said Nicky, picking it up. 'Oh!' said Nicky, when he found that the back wheels had fallen off. Quickly he put all the bits back on the window sill and hurried out of the room.

When Martin came home from school it wasn't long before there was trouble. 'Mum!' he shouted, as he dashed downstairs. 'Look at my car, it's broken!'

'Oh *dear*,' said Mummy. 'Now how did that happen?' She looked at Nicky. 'Do you know anything about it?'

'No!' said Nicky quickly, his cheeks going hot.

'Yes, he does!' shouted Martin. 'I bet he does!'

'I *don't!*' Nicky shouted back, his cheeks getting pinker.

'I expect it was Panda. She's always walking on the window sills.'

'That cat!' growled Martin, and he stamped off. This was *awful*. Nicky knew he was telling lies, and he knew he'd been naughty, but Martin was *so* cross, and now poor Panda was getting the blame, and it wasn't her fault at all. Nicky felt very uncomfortable. He had a sort of pain in his middle which wasn't a tummy ache.

Martin was very grumpy during tea. He wouldn't talk to Nicky or even watch his favourite TV programmes. Nicky didn't eat much tea – he still had that strange ache.

'Are you feeling all right?' asked Mummy. 'You've hardly touched your tea, and I thought you liked shepherd's pie.'

'I do, but I don't feel like it today,' Nicky mumbled. 'Can I get down? I don't want any

pudding.'

'OK,' said Mummy, and she gave him a funny look.

By bedtime Nicky had almost forgotten about the broken car, but then, there it was, sitting on the window sill when he went up to bed.

Oh dear, there was that strange feeling again. He stood and looked and looked at the model car. Mummy came quietly into the room.

'Hello, Nicky, what are you staring at?' Nicky jumped.

'I wish the wheels hadn't broken,' he said. 'I only brummed it very gently,' and he started to cry.

Mummy put her arms round him. 'Why didn't you tell the truth straight away?'

'Because Ma-Ma-Martin was so *cross*, and it's been a hor-hor-horrible day.' Poor Nicky. He cried and cried.

Then Mummy dried his face and he felt a bit better.

'Oh dear. We all have bad days sometimes. It's not your fault; some days just seem to be like that. But you made it worse. You were naughty to touch Martin's car, weren't you?' Nicky nodded. 'And you told a lie,' Nicky nodded and sniffed. 'It doesn't feel nice when you tell lies, does it?' Nicky remembered the ache in his middle, and nodded again. 'In the Bible God tells us we should always speak the truth to each other and not let the day finish with us still feeling angry. So, let's go and finish the day happily by telling the truth now.

Let's go and find Martin.'

They found Martin, and Nicky told him what

had happend, and that he was sorry, and Martin wasn't cross and didn't shout any more. After that Nicky felt *much* better – the ache had gone! Then he went and found Panda and gave her a 'sorry' stroke.

Later, Nicky was sitting in bed, eating his pudding off a tray. He didn't usually do this, but when the ache had gone it had left a big space and Nicky had felt very hungry. So mummy had let him have a special bedtime picnic.

He watched while Daddy helped Martin glue the wheels back on the model car. Martin was laughing and chatting happily, and Nicky felt that the day hadn't been quite so bad, after all. At least it had ended happily and he was going to make sure that tomorrow was a much better day!

Nicky and the new friend

One Monday morning Nicky was up bright and early, and so was everyone else in his house! He could hardly wait till the hands of his clock crept round to seven. Then he bounced out of bed and started to dress at once. Big brother Martin was still waking up on the top bunk.

'Be quiet, Nicky,' he yawned.

'It's school today. I don't want to be late,' answered Nicky.

'Well, you've got your vest on inside out *and* back-to-front,' said Martin, as he jumped to the floor.

It took a while to sort out the vest. Nicky always had trouble with dressing when he was excited or in a hurry.

This morning he was excited *and* in a hurry because today was his first day at school. Now that Nicky was almost five he was too old for Playgroup and he was ready to start school.

Edward and Charlene, his Playgroup friends, were starting too. They had all been on a special visit to see their class-room and to meet Mrs Lawson, their teacher. She had shown them all round and now they knew where all the toys were kept and where the toilets were.

Nicky's eyes had grown round when he caught sight of a big box of Lego in the cupboard. It was *huge* – much bigger than the one he and Martin had. Just think of all the cars and lorries he could make with that! He was so keen to start school that he had asked every evening, 'Is it school tomorrow?' and eventually Mummy had said, 'Yes. . . . tomorrow!' So now Nicky could put on his school clothes at last.

He had some special new things, like a jumper that Mummy had knitted, and a big bag to put his PE kit in.

He also had a bright red lunch box, with a drink bottle inside, just like Martin's. He wouldn't need it just yet, though, because the very new children came home at lunch-time for a few days.

After breakfast Nicky put his shoes and jacket on, without being asked once and he hopped about at the front door, while Martin cleaned his teeth and looked for his tie and his PE shorts.

'Come on, come on, come ON!' he begged. 'We'll be late!'

'Oh no, we won't,' laughed Mummy, as she collected her keys and shopping bag. 'I don't think Mrs Lawson wants to see us yet. She'll still be getting organized.'

'Well, I'm organized *now*. Martin, please come on!'

At last they were on their way. All along the road they saw other children going to school. Children with dads, children with mums and babies in prams, children in cars, big children going on their own. Martin knew lots of them and soon he met some of his friends and was chattering happily. Nicky held Mummy's hand and thought about the big box of Lego.

At the school gate Martin said goodbye and hurried off to his class-room while Mummy and Nicky went to find Mrs Lawson. Outside the class-room Nicky suddenly felt shy.

There were quite a few children there already. They were dong jigsaw puzzles and looking at books. Nicky spied the Lego on a table, and pulled Mummy into the room.

'Hello, Nicky,' said Mrs Lawson. 'Can you remember where to hang your jacket and bag?' Nicky nodded. 'Good. Well, when you come back, you can choose something to do.' In no time Nicky was busy building a police car.

'Well, I'll go and do my shopping now,' said Mummy. 'See you at lunch-time. Be good!' She gave him a kiss and off she went. Soon Edward arrived and then Charlene, and they all played together.

Then Mrs Lawson called the children to the big mat and they all introduced themselves. After that they had a story and some songs, and then it was playtime. Nicky, Edward and Charlene stayed together and went into the playground. It was *very* noisy and seemed full of children. Mrs Lawson showed them where to play, near the class-room, so that they didn't get mixed up with the big children. Then she came out with a little boy. 'Nicky, would you and your friends look after Stefan for me? He's only just moved to our town and he doesn't know anybody yet.' Stefan was very quiet and didn't seem to want to do anything, so they

all sat on the class-room steps and watched the bigger children running and shouting.

Martin dashed past. 'You OK, Nick?' he asked.

Nicky nodded and grinned. 'Good,' said Martin and away he ran.

'That's my big brother,' said Nicky proudly.

'I've got a brother too,' said Stefan. 'He's in this school, but I don't know where,' and he looked sad.

'Your mum will get you soon,' said Charlene. 'We all go home at lunch-time.' Nicky and Edward nodded.

'I've got a lunch-box for when I stay at school all day,' said Nicky.

'So've I,' said Edward. 'Mine's got robots on it.

'Mine hasn't got pictures but it's *very* yellow,' said Charlene.

'I like robots,' said Stefan. 'Look,' and he pulled a toy robot out of his pocket.

'Wow! Let's have a look!' said Nicky and the others. Stefan let them each have a turn holding it. 'I got it for my birthday,' he explained. 'I'm five now. I had a party at my old house.'

'I'm going to be five soon,' said Nicky. 'I'd like a robot like this.'

When the bell rang Mrs Lawson called them all inside.

Stefan stayed close to Nicky. Mrs Lawson asked them all to draw a picture of their news and write about it underneath. She said, 'Don't worry if you can't write stories yet. I'll help you.' Nicky was glad about that because he could only just write his name. Mrs Lawson wrote his story and he copied it underneath. It was hard work! Nicky looked at Stefan, who was sitting next to him. He was really writing. Nicky was impressed. Stefan is clever, he thought.

The rest of the morning passed quickly and soon the children were collecting their coats, and there were their mums to meet them. Nicky bounded up to his mummy, flapping his news-picture around his head. 'Did you have a good time?' she asked. Nicky nodded.

'We worked hard, but we played too. I wrote this, and that's Stefan. He hasn't got any friends.' He pointed at Stefan who was walking across the playground with his mummy. Stefan's mummy smiled at Nicky.

'Stefan says that you and your friends looked after him today. Thank you *very* much, Nicky.' Then the two mummies talked, while Nicky and Stefan looked at Stefan's robot again.

Later, as they walked home, Mummy said, 'Stefan didn't want to come to school today because he wouldn't know anyone. He left all his friends where he used to live and he was lonely.'

'I wasn't lonely,' said Nicky. 'I know Edward and Charlene. We all looked after Stefan.'

'Well, that's lovely,' said Mummy. 'Stefan's mummy wants to know if you'd like to play at their house one day. They don't live far from us.'

Nicky skipped and smiled to himself. A new school, a new teacher, new things to do, and a new friend, all in one day! He could hardly wait until tomorrow.

Nicky's happy birthday party

'Happy birthday to you,
Happy birthday to you,
Happy birthday dear Nicky,
Happy birthday to you!!'

It was Nicky's birthday *at last*. He'd been counting
the weeks on the kitchen calendar, then the days.
Three weeks, two weeks, one week . . . six
days . . . 5 . . . 4 . . . 3 . . . 2 . . . 1. Hooray!
Now he was five. The whole family crowded into
Mummy and Daddy's bed, ready for Nicky to
open his presents. It was rather early in the
morning, but Nicky hadn't been able to wait any
longer. Just this once Mummy and Daddy hadn't
grumbled when he'd crept into their room before
the alarm went off.

First they had sung Happy Birthday to him, and
now Daddy handed him his parcels one by one.
There was much rustling and ripping of paper and
lots of ohs and thank yous. Soon the bed was
covered in brightly-coloured paper, and Nicky had
a heap of lovely presents.

There was a really big Lego set from Mummy
and Daddy, roller skates from Auntie Liz, felt pens

from big brother Martin, a sweater from Grannie, books, toy cars, games, paints. . . . the list went on and on. Nicky didn't know what to look at first. Martin helped him to carry everything into their bedroom, and then they began to unpack the Lego. But they didn't play for long because soon Mummy was calling them for breakfast and it was time for school.

'I wish I could stay home today and play with my presents,' said Nicky.

'If you stayed home today you wouldn't have time to play,' said Mummy with a laugh. 'You'd have to help me. I've got *so* much to do for your party this afternoon!'

Nicky brightened up as he thought about his party. It was going to be a pirate party. He and Martin had been working hard to make pirate hats out of black paper for everyone.

'Is my pirate suit ready?' Nicky asked.

'It will be by this afternoon. Now, eat that toast and let's be on our way,' said Mummy.

The day seemed to pass very slowly for Nicky but, eventually, the end-of-school bell rang and Mummy hurried him and Martin home to do the final preparations before the children arrived at tea-time. Nicky shivered with excitement as he and Martin struggled into their stripey shirts, baggy trousers and eye patches. Then they dashed downstairs to help.

Daddy had come home early, especially for the party, and he and Martin got to work pushing the sitting-room furniture against the wall. This was to make room for the games. Nicky wandered into the kitchen and found Mummy putting the finishing touches to the party food. He had been able to choose what they would eat, and there were many of his favourite things; crisps, potato rings, cheese spread sandwiches, little buns, chocolate finger biscuits, red and green jelly and some special 'Yo-ho-ho Pirate Drink' that Mummy had invented.

Auntie Liz had made the birthday cake because she was good at that sort of thing. It was a little chocolate pirate ship with sweets for the treasure and knitting needle masts with sails made of special paper that she said you could really eat! It all looked *very* nice.

'I'm hungry,' said Nicky.

'Just a few crisps then,' said Mummy. Then there was a 'bing-bong' at the door bell and the first children were arriving.

All Nicky's friends were there: Edward, Charlene and Stefan from school, Lucy-down-the-road and several others from his old Playgroup and from Sunday school, too. They were all dressed like pirates, and each one had brought a present. There was more rustling paper and *more* ohs and thank yous. Then it was time for the games.

First they played Musical Bumps. 'When the music stops, the last one to sit down is out!' Daddy explained. Nicky and Stefan were the best, but then Stefan won. Nicky was cross.

'It's not fair!' he grumbled. 'I was first to sit down.'

'No, you weren't,' said Daddy. 'Stefan was quicker.'

Nicky stuck out his bottom lip and flumped into an armchair.

'Now it's Pass-the-Parcel,' Mummy announced loudly.

'Yay!' cheered the children, and Nicky bounded out of his chair to join the circle on the floor. The music played and round and round went the parcel, getting smaller and smaller. Twice Nicky had a turn of unwrapping, but he didn't get the prize. It was Lucy who won. Again Nicky was annoyed.

'I wanted to win,' he whined. 'It's *my* birthday.'

'You've had lots of presents, Nick,' Martin reminded him.

The games continued, and each time someone else won a prize Nicky grew more cross and sulky. Then it was teatime and it became very quiet as the children began to eat. Nicky was trying to fit a potato ring on each of his fingers. He grabbed the last few, just as Charlene reached for some.

'Just a minute,' said Daddy. 'You've got lots already. Give some to Charlene.'

'No,' Nicky growled.

'Put them back, and come with me!' Daddy said firmly, and he marched Nicky out of the room. 'Now look here. We've had a bit too much of "I want" and "me first" this afternoon.'

'But it's my birthday,' was the grumpy reply.

'Yes, but we all want to enjoy it with you. If you win *all* the games and eat most of the food it's not much fun for the rest of us. Not a party at all really.'

Nicky kicked at the carpet with his toe. 'It's not being a very happy party', he grumbled.

'Happiness needs to be shared. It doesn't last very long if you keep it to yourself. I think you'll enjoy your party much more if you let everyone share your happy day.'

Nicky sighed. He knew Daddy was right. He hadn't been enjoying his party very much because he'd been too busy trying to keep everything for himself.

'Time to blow out your candles,' Mummy called as Nicky came back into the room. There was the pirate ship, lit up with five candles. After the children had sung Happy Birthday he blew out all the candles in one puff, and then handed pieces of cake to each of his friends in turn. He made sure that everyone got the same number of treasure sweets.

Then there were more games, and Nicky didn't complain when another child won. When it was time for his friends to go home, he didn't push or grab for the best balloon.

Afterwards Mummy and Daddy flopped into chairs for a rest, and the boys went to see if there was any food left.

'That was a good party,' said Martin, his mouth full of red jelly.

'Yes, it was . . . in the end,' Nicky agreed. He pulled at one of the paper sails and nibbled the edge. He'd had some lovely presents and a super party, really. And yes, it was more fun when you let other people enjoy themselves. Mmmm, you really could eat this paper stuff! He was just going to put the whole big bit into his mouth, when he stopped.

'Have some of this, Martin. It's nice,' he said, and they enjoyed it together.

Being glad

It was playtime at school, and Nicky's class was out in the sunshine, running and shouting, scrambling over the climbing frame or sitting on the classroom steps. Nicky and his friends, Stefan and Charlene, and some other children from their class were busy making a house by the hedge in the corner of their part of the playground. They had begun to scratch the outline of the walls in the dust, and now some of them were collecting little stones to cover the scratched lines. They chattered happily as they worked. Edward wandered up. 'Can I play?' he asked.

'Yes,' Nicky replied. He was still busily scratching lines with a long, pointy stick. The lines had begun to be a picture of a car. Nicky was enjoying himself.

'Give me the stick,' said Edward.

'No,' answered Nicky. 'You get more stones.'

'I don't want to. Give me the stick!' Edward grabbed at the stick in Nicky's hand.

'No, Edward,' Nicky protested. 'I'm using it. You can have it when I'm finished.'

'Give it me *now!*' shouted Edward, and he punched Nicky in the arm. Nicky was surprised.

'Ow! That hurt!' It wasn't like Edward to go hitting like that. Edward scowled at Nicky and tried to push him over.

'Give me that stick!' he shouted.

Now Nicky was upset. What was the matter with Edward? Usually they were such good friends. They hardly ever quarrelled. He didn't really care about the stick, so he dropped it on the ground.

'There you are then! I'm telling my dad about you!'

'Don't care,' said Edward, as he picked up the stick. Charlene ran up with more stones, and Nicky began to arrange them along the lines. Edward stabbed and poked at the ground with the stick. 'Will you really tell your dad?' he asked anxiously. Nicky didn't answer.

'I haven't got a dad any more,' Edward muttered.

Nicky was surprised again. 'Of *course* you have! Everyone has a dad!'

Edward swished the stick crossly. 'Well, he doesn't live at our house any more and my bike's broken and Mummy can't mend it.' He threw the stick high in the air and ran off down the playground.

Nicky knelt by his row of stones and thought and thought. No Daddy? No one to mend broken bikes and things. This was something new to him . . . Maybe that had something to do with Edward being so cross today.

At tea-time that evening Nicky said, 'Edward's daddy doesn't live at his house any more.'

'Yes, lovey, I knew,' said Mummy sadly.

'Edward hit me . . . he hasn't got his daddy to mend his bike. That's a bit sad, isn't it?' Mummy agreed that it was. 'I'm glad I've got a daddy,' Nicky continued, and big brother Martin nodded his head.

'We've got a lot to be glad about,' said Mummy. 'There are many children that haven't got Mummies or Daddies. There are lots of people that don't have the things that we have, like food and strong, healthy bodies . . .'

' . . . and houses to live in,' added Martin.

'Yes, that's right,' Mummy continued. 'Remember the pictures of the earthquake on television news yesterday?' Nicky thought about the fallen-down houses he'd seen and the children sleeping in tents.

'I like sleeping in a tent.'

'Tents are fun on holiday, but not in the winter,' said Martin. Nicky nodded slowly and thought again.

'I've got a daddy and a house that's not falling down and a bike that's not broken. That's a lot, isn't it?'

'It certainly is,' Mummy agreed. 'How about asking Edward to play after school tomorrow? You're good friends really, aren't you?'

'And he could ride my bike! He'd like that.'

'That would be a lovely idea,' said Mummy with a smile. 'God has given us such a lot to be glad about. We can share some of it with other people as a way of saying thank you to him.'

'Come on, eat up, Nick,' said Martin. 'I'll help you pump up your tyres ready for tomorrow.'

Nicky gulped down the last of his tea. I've got

a big brother, as well, he thought. I'm glad about
that too!

Nicky goes to the zoo

Nicky's class were going on a trip to the zoo. They were very excited, and this meant that they were very noisy. 'We're going to the zoo, zoo, zoo! How about you, you, you?' they sang as they waited at the school gate for the coach to arrive.

'Quiet everyone, and stand still while I count you,' Mrs Lawson called. She and the mothers who had come to help went along the line of children 'shush-ing' and making everyone stand still. But it was so hard not to jiggle about just a little bit.

At last the coach came and the children scrambled on board. Nicky found an empty seat, and Edward and Stefan squeezed into it with him.

'Three in a seat?' said one of the mothers. 'Won't you be squashed?'

'No, we don't care! We're friends!' laughed the boys. There was more counting and 'shush-ing' and then they were on their way.

Nicky enjoyed riding in the coach. They were so high up. You could see right over the cars, and smile at the lorry drivers in their cabs. You could see over fences and hedges too. It was much more interesting than riding in a car. It wasn't a long trip and, by the time they'd sung a few songs and played 'I-Spy', the coach was slowing down and creeping into its space in the zoo car park.

Then there was still more 'shush-ing' and counting while children were divided into little groups with their mothers, then at *last* they were able to go. Nicky and his friends were with two girls in Mrs Lawson's group. She made them stay close beside her as they went through the big gates. Then they stood and looked at the signposts with the pictures of animals that pointed to where the animals lived.

'I want to see the giraffes!'

'Let's go and find the parrots!'

'Can we buy an ice cream?'

Mrs Lawson laughed and said that they could all have turns of choosing what they wanted to see. 'Stefan, you may choose first.' Stefan chose the elephants. Nicky liked elephants too and they stood for a long time watching the huge animals as they strolled slowly round their enclosure. Their grey-brown skin was all saggy and folded and crusty. It looks far too big for them, Nicky thought. How enormous their feet were, but how quietly they could walk! One of the elephants picked up a stick with his trunk and clanged it on the fence. The children laughed, and another stretched out his trunk and 'phoofed' at them through the railings. The children backed away, not too sure about this.

'He's OK!' laughed a man in a peaked cap. 'He's just saying hello. Don't feed him though, will you? He has his own special food and we don't want him getting a tummy ache, do we?'

'No, indeed,' agreed Mrs Lawson. 'Such a big

animal would have a very big tummy ache!' and the children laughed again.

Next it was Nicky's turn and he chose the sea-lions. They lived in a big pond, as blue as the swimming pool at the sports centre, but a much more interesting shape. There were crowds of people here, and the children had to squeeze between grown-ups to get a good view.

'It's nearly feeding-time,' Mrs Lawson explained. The sea-lions were hungry and becoming impatient. They skimmed through the water and flopped out on to the rocks that surrounded their pool. They waggled their heads about, as if they were looking for someone, and then splash, back into the water they went again.

'They're waiting for their dinner,' said Edward.

Suddenly another man in a peaked cap and green wellies came through the gate. He was carrying a big bucket. Now the sea-lions became very excited. The people leaned over the fence to get a better view. Nicky and the other children felt rather squashed, but they didn't mind. One big sea-lion sat up on a rock clapping his flippers together. 'Ark! Ark! Ark!' he shouted. The keeper tossed him a silver fish and, 'gulp!' it was gone in a flash. The children squealed with delight. Again and again the keeper tossed the fish and each time the sea-lions caught them. They never dropped one!

And all the time there was the 'Ark! Ark! Ark!' and the splashing and the laughing. It was a *very* noisy meal. When the keeper's bucket was empty the sea-lions grew quiet and slipped back into the water to swim slowly and gently. Nicky thought they were lovely. He wished *he* could swim under water like they did.

Gradually the crowds of people drifted away and Nicky could look around him. It was then that he realised he was alone. Mrs Lawson and the others were nowhere to be seen!

Oh, thought Nicky. Now what? He wasn't sure whether to be frightened or not. There were still so many people, and the zoo was such a big place. Where could the others have gone? Perhaps they'd gone to see the giraffes? Should he go that way? Then he remembered what Mummy had said he must do if he ever lost her at the shops. 'Stand still and wait for me to find you.' So Nicky stayed where he was and looked about him. There were lots of people, but no one he recognized. All the time he was thinking. What if Mrs Lawson doesn't know she's lost me? What if they have lunch without me? Nicky grew worried. What if they go home without me? I mustn't move, he thought, but he felt very lonely. I wish Edward was here, or Stefan, he thought . . . but – Jesus is with me. The thought seemed to just pop into his head. Mummy had said that Jesus had promised never to leave us, and that even though we can't see him he's always very near.

Now Nicky felt a little better. Still there were all these people and no one that he knew. 'Jesus will look after me,' he said to himself.

'Nicky! Oh *there* you are!' It was Mrs Lawson with all the other children from the group scurrying along behind her. She looked worried. Would she be cross, Nicky wondered.

'We nearly reached the giraffes when we realized that you weren't with us. We must have been separated in the crowds. What a sensible boy you were to stay still and wait for us to find you.' Nicky was glad that Mrs Lawson wasn't cross and even more glad to be back with his group again. 'Well now. I think we'll join the others for lunch, and we'll visit the giraffes afterwards,' said Mrs Lawson brightly. 'Oh, and Nicky, you can hold my hand. I don't want to lose you again!'

For the rest of the day Nicky stayed very close to Mrs Lawson and his group and they all had a lovely time. When they arrived back at school all the mums and dads were there to meet them. Nicky could hardly wait to tell Mummy about his day. He told her about being high up in the coach, about the funny elephant, and the noisy sea-lion meal. . . . 'Oh and I got lost too,' he added.

'Were you frightened?' asked Mummy.

'Mmm, a bit,' Nicky admitted, 'but Jesus was with me so we waited until Mrs Lawson found us. She was quite quick and she wasn't cross and we all had an ice lolly.'

'It sounds as though you've had an exciting time,' Mummy said. 'The end-of-school bell has gone, so let's go and find Martin now and tell him about your adventures.'

And that's the story of what happened when Nicky went to the zoo.